Many thanks to Amy, Chris, Kaylan, and Caroline

Copyright © 2007 by Randy Cecil

First edition 2007

Library of Congress Cataloging-in-Publication Data

Cecil, Randy.
Gator / Randy Cecil. —1st ed.
p. cm.
Summary: When the amusement park where
he had been a happy carousel animal closes, Gator decides
to explore the outside world but finds it a very lonely place.
ISBN 978-0-7636-2952-6
[1. Alligators —Fiction. 2. Merry-go-round —Fiction.
3. Amusement parks —Fiction.] I. Title.
PZ7 . C2999Gat 2007
[E] —dc22   2006047556

2 4 6 8 10 9 7 5 3 1

Printed in Singapore

This book was typeset in Malonia Voigo.
The illustrations were done in oil.

Candlewick Press
2067 Massachusetts Avenue
Cambridge, Massachusetts 02140

visit us at www.candlewick.com

GATOR

Randy Cecil

CANDLEWICK PRESS
CAMBRIDGE, MASSACHUSETTS

Gator was once the happiest carousel animal
in the world. He loved the flashing lights, the sound
of the calliope, and the feeling of wind on his face.
But most of all, he loved the laughter.

In those days, the line for the carousel seemed to go on forever. All the children wanted to ride on Gator, Duck, or the Golden Fish.

But times had changed.
Every day the crowd was smaller
than the day before.

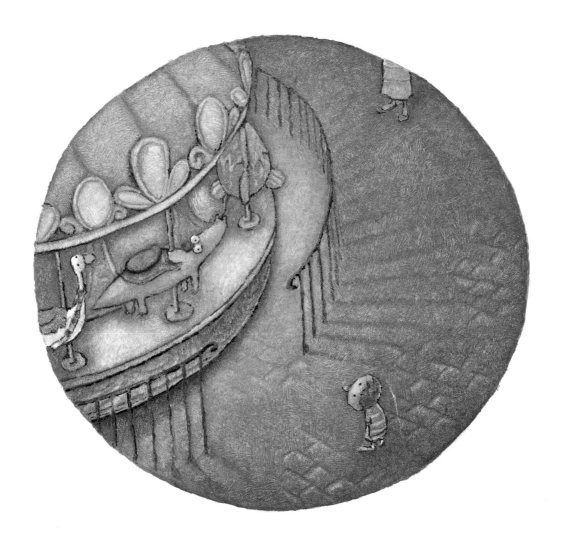

Finally, the amusement park was all but forgotten.
The rides stopped running, the lights went dark,
and the laughter was gone. With nothing else to do,
Gator fell into a deep sleep.

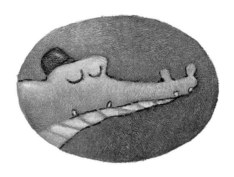

He slept and he slept.

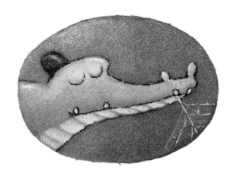

And as he slept, he dreamed that
he was once again whirling on the carousel.
He could even feel the wind on his face.

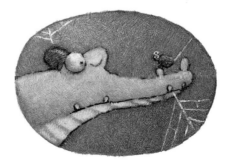

But it was only a spider attaching its web
to his snout. The carousel was still quiet.
The park was still empty.

Unable to sleep any longer, Gator left his place on the carousel. He touched the hole in his heart where the pole had been and looked out over the empty park. It was time to leave.

"But where will you go?" asked Duck.
"I'm not sure," Gator said.

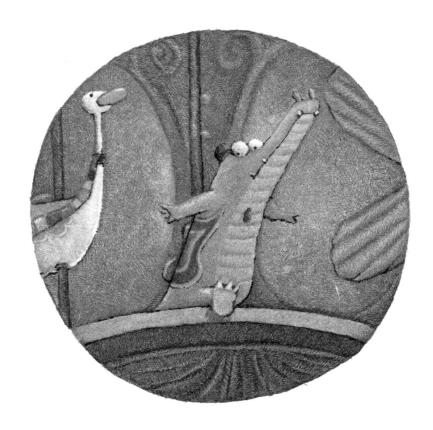

When he reached the park gate, he turned around and looked back at the carousel, where he had spent his entire life. He looked at Duck, his friend who had always been there, right behind him.

Then Gator opened the gate and
walked out into the world.

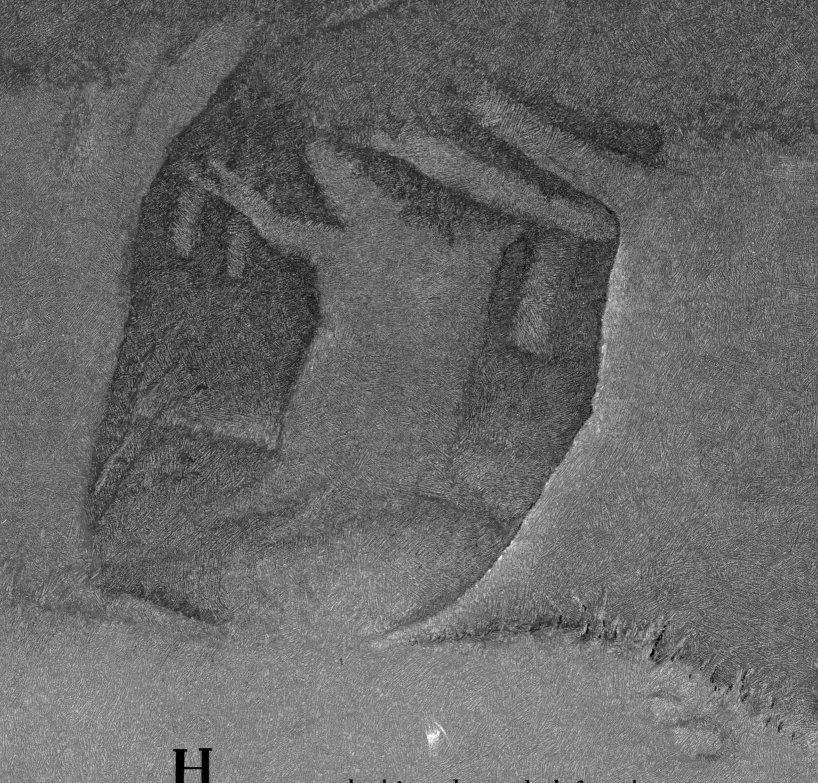

He was soon lost in a deep, dark forest.
He walked and walked until he knew every turn in
every path, every twist in every tree. A cold wind
blew through the hole in Gator's heart.

At last he came to a bridge. Some ducks
were swimming in the stream below.
"Well, look at that!" Gator said. "They look
just like my friend Duck."

He leaned over to say hello with his biggest,
friendliest, toothiest smile.

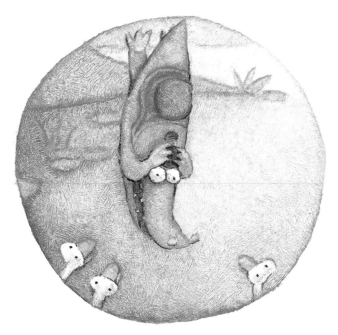

But he slipped, so instead of saying hello,
he said something more like "AAAGHEEEE!"

And the ducks flew away.

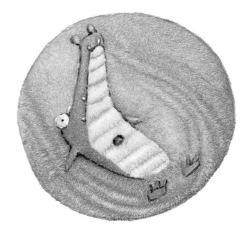

Gator hadn't known
that ducks could fly.
"How amazing!

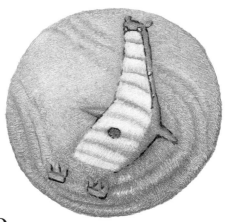

I'll have to
remember to tell Duck
about that."

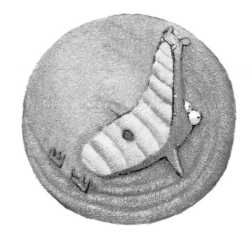

And then Gator heard something.

Laughter! It was coming from beyond a large open gate. "Maybe this is some sort of amusement park!" Gator said as he walked inside.

But where were the flashing lights?

Where was the calliope?

Just as Gator began to think that it
was not an amusement park after all,
he saw something amazing.
"Alligators!" he gasped.
"Maybe I should go in and say hello."

But they were not what he had imagined.
These alligators were big. These alligators were scary.
Luckily, they were also asleep.

Quickly, Gator tiptoed back out of the alligator pen.

Tears filled his eyes. He was tired
and lonely, and his search had led him nowhere.
He sat down on a bench and began to cry. He had
had enough. He wanted to go home.

Then Gator heard a little boy laughing.
"Daddy, what's that funny alligator doing
out here?" asked the boy.
"Why, that's no alligator," said the boy's father.
"That's Gator! He was my favorite animal
on the carousel at the old amusement park."
"Can we go there?" the little boy asked.
"I want to ride on Gator."

Gator jumped up. The amusement park hadn't been forgotten! He could bring the laughter back. He began to lead the way to the carousel. He was going home! More and more people followed.

On and on they went, back over the bridge and through the forest.

"Hello, Duck!" called Gator as he led
the people through the gates.

The calliope began to play, and the lights came back on.

Gator took his place on the carousel,
and the little boy climbed up on his back.
The hole in Gator's heart was gone.

He turned to tell Duck about his many adventures.
Did she know that ducks could fly?

As the carousel whirled around,
laughter filled the amusement park.
Everything was just the way
it used to be....

Except for Duck!